Break Me

Break Me

Tom Reynolds

QUATTRO BOOKS

The publication of *Break Me* has been generously supported by the Canada Council for the Arts and the Ontario Arts Council.

Canada Council for the Arts Conseil des Arts du Canada

ONTARIO ARTS COUNCIL
CONSEIL DES ARTS DE L'ONTARIO

Cover art: Portion of *Self-Portrait* by Egon Schiele
Cover design: Diane Mascherin
Typography: Grey Wolf Typography
Editor: John Calabro

Library and Archives Canada Cataloguing in Publication

Reynolds, Tom
Break me / Tom Reynolds.

ISBN 978-1-926802-32-9

I. Title.

PS8635.E949B74 2011 C813'.6 C2010-907667-2

Novella Series #19
Published by Quattro Books Inc.
89 Pinewood Avenue, Toronto, Ontario, M6C 2V2
www.quattrobooks.ca

Printed in Canada

One

I am thirty-nine years old and my mother just died. At last, my life can begin.

✵

I use the money left to me in the will to self-publish a book of essays and take them round to the shops that sell books. I offer, in my magnanimous way, to give it to them for free, so all it will cost them is a bit of shelf space, but even that is too much for them to give up. They all say no to me. So I publish it on the web, for anyone to see or read or copy or plagiarize, and that earns me some e-mails, such as:

> *You are to die and burn hell [sic]. You are fucked.*
> *You should die. Fuck you.*

Or this:

> *Who told you you could write? My ten year old got an A+ on a story about his dog. That's real writing. I'd rather read the story about his dog my ten year old wrote.*

Or this:

Increase your pen1s 3x guaranteed.

It doesn't matter. I have killed the only woman I have ever loved.

❋

I remember reading a library book once that said love was the meaning of life. There is a song you hear on the radio all the time about a woman and her boyfriend and how good their sex life is. I pass a church everyday on my bicycle and I know that if I went inside they would tell me God loves me. The things people believe.

❋

All a man wants, all a man asks, all a man demands is that the pain go away. Just that. The simple, direct, emotional, psychological, spiritual pain. We are not bothered by our own smallness in comparison to the universe, the certainty of our own death, or our vulnerability to random events like earthquakes or cancer. Does anyone actually commit suicide out of angst at the realization that the average life span is seventy-five, or because the earth is just a speck in a corner off to one side of an unfathomably large cosmos? Or do people commit suicide because they are in pain, and the only way they can imagine the pain ending is if everything ends? Death, the one great hope. They are wrong, of course. Suicides go to hell. It's obvious. This is because death does not end pain. There are some pains that are so deep they go on even after death. There are some loves so strong you can die and still be in love. This is because love and pain are the same thing. Does anyone doubt it?

❋

"Pierre."

I say nothing.

"Pierre."

"What?"

"It is incredible – that you should feel that way. I am flattered, but it's not like that."

I have not spoken because I want anything or had any hope. If I had been accepted I would have rejected the acceptance. I am merely conducting an experiment to see how deep unhappiness can go, an experiment to see how unhappy I can make myself. If Jackie had accepted me I would have been disgusted.

It occurs to me that it is not my fault. It is God's. There are people who believe in God and say that he is loving and kind. There are people who do not believe in God at all. What you never hear is someone who believes in God, but thinks he is a malicious, spiteful, sadistic, bastard God, or a confused, incompetent, weak-brained, foolish God and a poor manager of human resources.

If the good things in life are evidence of God's love, are not the bad things in life evidence of God's vindictiveness or incompetence? Is the glass half empty or half full? Or is it, as one wag said, twice as large as it needs to be? Drink the drink down, and let us smash the glass against the fireplace. As the Greeks say, "Let the games begin."

Two

It is a far, far better thing I think than I have ever thought before, so listen: Into a lifeless world life emerges, but the pre-life world gains no advantage from life. The life which emerges gains no advantage from its emergence, from its being alive, over that of its not being alive, because existence and non-existence are not categories that can be compared with respect to a thing. There is no non-existent being a living being can be compared to. Once I am a living human I may be able to imagine not existing, but that is imagination, rhetoric; any advantage I may think existing has is not an advantage over not existing but an advantage over existing in a different way. To experience beauty or love I must exist, but these are not advantages over not existing, but over existing, but for psychological or circumstantial reasons being unable to experience them. If I did not exist there would be no me to experience my lack of existence as a loss. There would be no me to experience not loving, not seeing beauty, as a loss. Likewise this extends to all life, to the idea of life, to capital-L life; if Life did not exist, there would be no life to experience the lack of Life as a loss.

How happy, someone said, we could be in a world in which we did not exist. And to that we all say, "Amen, amen."

I am in my bare feet. I am looking at the floor. It is a good floor. It has supported me my whole life. I am in my pyjamas. I am looking at the window. It is a good window. It has shown me the moon my whole life. I am looking in the mirror. It is a magic mirror. It has shown me some stranger's face my whole life.

If a man wanted to be understood, what would he write?

Three

People must recognize that they do not know me. This is because a) I am a secret, and b) because no one knows anyone. On the news there is talk of a politician's sex life. It is always surprising to think of politicians having sex lives. There is a war on someplace. Africa, perhaps – there is always a war on in Africa. Climate change is killing the earth. There have always been birds that kill mosquitoes, now there are mosquitoes that kill birds. We are told by the health department to report any dead jays or crows we find so they can be tested for West Nile Virus. I called to report one once and they were very rude. I will not do it again.

But, one worries. In the face of this world, in the teeth of this life, what value is there in someone knowing another person? If someone falls in love with someone else it does not make either of them a better person, or solve the homeless problem in Jonquiere. We do not give more to charity because we are happily married or engaged – they've done studies. It is not easy opposing love, sex, war, God, work, the government, polluters, and literary critics; it is not easy being a thinking man. It is not easy being.

❋

"Pierre," John says to me, "I see you're putting up posters."

John begins every conversation by taking whatever he sees you doing and forming a sentence about it. "Pierre," he says, "I see you are out for a walk," or "Pierre, you have a bandage on your hand," or "Pierre, I see you're putting up posters."

"Yes," I say. "Do you know that forty thousand children die every day from preventable diseases?"

"Really? No, I did not know that. Well, well, well. That's not very good is it? Still, the bakery might not appreciate having that poster stuck smack dab in the middle of their window."

People always expect me to be concerned about the strangest things.

"It's a place people will see it," I say.

"Yes, yes. Still, maybe you should go home, have yourself a nice cup of tea." John is a silly man. There is nothing for me at home.

There is a tide in the affairs of men which when waded into in bare feet will cut, bruise, sore the soles on the stones and thorns and fish of the jelly kind. There. Who says I can't write? I go down to the beach – you have to go down an incline – to look for insects and bugs. There are always some there. Sand fleas, spiders, bees, hornets, flies. The one thing I can say about my house for certain is that there are no bugs. I make sure of that. Anything I see I kill and I have the man around to spray every three months. If there is going to be anything alive in my house, it should be me. Or Guy.

I remember reading in another library book that people used to believe in Spontaneous Generation, that is, that life came – pop! – out of nowhere. If you shot a Zebra and left it there and came back later there would be maggots in it. Where did they come from? How does a dead animal give birth to live animals? How does life come out of death?

Someone did an experiment and showed that tiny flies laid eggs in the carcass and that was where the maggots came from. It is obvious to us, but it had to be figured out. Life comes from other life, which means there must have always been life, since there has been time. When God dies – truly dies, not rhetorically dies, as in Nietzsche – time will end, life will end. That is the meaning of eternal life. It is nonsense, of course. I do not believe.

Riding down the sidewalk slowly I see Jackie and her new boyfriend sitting at an outside table at the Cocky Rooster sipping coffees. Jackie is a fine woman, the men all say so, but it is difficult to know what the word 'fine' means. I think it means they think she'd make a good wife, although it is difficult to know what the word 'good' means. I think it means that they want to sleep with her, though by 'sleep' I think they mean insert themselves into her physically over and over anytime they want. But I've been through her trash. I know what she's really like.

"Pierre," Gerald the boyfriend says to me, "how goes it?"

"Yes, Pierre," Jackie says, "how are you?"

How am I at what? I wonder. Is she flirting with me?

"Do you know," Gerald says, "I was thinking of you the other day. The library has posted a job looking for a janitor. Part-time, I imagine. Still, it would be quiet."

Why he thinks I require quiet I do not know.

"May I have a croissant?" I say. "I'm hungry. I haven't eaten."

They order me one. I do not sit down.

"Pity about the Spartans," Gerald says.

I do not follow sports.

"You're looking tanned," Jackie says to me. I walk or bicycle everywhere; of course I look tanned. I shrug.

"Would you like a coffee?"

"Coffee's bad for my nerves," I say. "Besides, it kills brain cells."

Something has changed. Jackie has always been an attractive middle-aged woman living alone in the house her dead father built out of boards. He and her mother divorced. She has always had male friends – so naturally there were rumours. There are always rumours. There were rumours about me, after all, so it's not surprising there should be rumours about her. But the rumours about her tended to be about her body. Nobody whispered she was a secret alcoholic, or had money stolen from her mother hidden away, or killed stray cats.

Guns – I won't have them in the house. That's what the tool shed is for.

I eat my croissant when it comes and continue on my mission down the avenue to the mission, but I do not go in. It is hard, it is very hard, to think of myself as one of them. It is actually easier for me to identify with the enormously wealthy than the terribly poor and homeless, though I am oh so much more close to being the latter. How did I develop this identification with the oppressor class over the oppressed? I do not know. I think I blame television. That is why I fight so hard for the poor in Asia and Africa, the orphans and the sick, the babies, the mothers, the old people – because I know in my heart I am not one of them. It is compensation for my envy of the priests and the barons and the businessmen and the blessed emptiness of their lives, the blessed, blessed freedom from reality that I long for myself. Sometimes my imagination carries me away. I have thought up a scene for a movie: a young man is picking up his new girlfriend for the first time, and he pulls up in an old, beat-up junker of a car. The woman, who is well-dressed, looks at the car sceptically. "I know it's not much of a car," the young man says, "but I'm compensating for my enormous penis."

That is something else I envy. No, not envy, envy is but another name for fear and I am not afraid, of myself, or of my lot, or of my future. My inadequacies give me opportunities. If I were good-looking I'd be wasting my time on women, night after night. If I were athletic I'd be playing football and weightlifting and drinking. If I were intelligent (or more so than I am, or less so) I would spend all day reading books and documents. My being me presents me with the opportunity to live a life I could not live any other way. I eat little, I do not smoke or drink, I do not gamble or go to church. I have not created any life where there was not one before – no one can turn to me and say, "Why did you have me? I wish I was never born." No woman can divorce me and take half my house. I will never be cheated by a used car salesman because I will never have a car. I will never go to war, not even if the Germans or the Jamaicans come and point their guns at my next door neighbour's head. I would rather die than fight. I would rather be ugly and weak and stupid and alone and poor, than not be me.

❋

Leticia is a little girl. Leticia is my friend. Sometimes we sit in the sun on the curb in front of her uncle's house by the field of weeds next to Turkey Creek, and she talks to me about her knees or her stomach aches or why there is water.

"The reason there is water," she says, "is because the grass needs it."

So there you go, faith such as a little child has. It is the need that calls forth the blessing. Because it is needed, it is there. Because it would be wrong for it not to be there.

"We have more fresh water here than anyone in the world," I say.

"Yes," she says.

I immediately regret saying that, because I remember her mother had drowned at sea, which was honestly not on my mind when I said we have more fresh water here than any other country in the world.

"I'm sorry about your mother," I say. "The water took her, didn't it?"

"My uncle says I can get my revenge by drinking a glass of water everyday. But I don't want revenge."

"What do you want, Leticia? Your mother?"

"I want," Leticia says, "to grow up," and she stands, picks up a stone and throws it into the creek.

"There," she says.

Leticia's father is in Afghanistan and she lives with her uncle Jacob, who is a large *Bonhomme* fellow, but given to outbursts of anger and strength. Charming in many ways, he makes what he says is Absinthe in his basement. No one I know has ever tried it or seen it, or admitted that they have tried or seen it. There is a rumour going about that he is involved with a motorcycle gang, and at times it seems just possible, but most of the time it seems absurd. He is a painter, or claims to be – an artist. He has read widely, to judge from his conversation. He speaks French and English, and he drives a Corsair. At one time it must have been vintage, but now it is just a car, neither immaculate nor a wreck. He is always nice to me.

Leticia sometimes speaks to me of a man who is her friend, her other grown-up friend. She tells me how much he loves animals and how he thinks animals are people waiting to be born. The only animals she likes, she says, are turtles because everything is slow to them and they can hide inside themselves. I tell her about chameleons, which can hide by changing colour, but she does not believe me.

"A leopard cannot change its spots," she says. Which, alas, I have to admit is true.

❋

Some of us are prematurely old, and philosophy is the consolation of the elderly. If one had never been born one would never be able to experience any of the happiness or pleasure one gets a chance at in life, but since one was never born, one can hardly be said to feel their absence as a loss. One would not only not experience pleasure, but would also not experience the desire for pleasure that makes fulfilling that desire pleasurable. Yes, a person would never know the satisfaction of a well-prepared meal; but one would never know the hunger or the bodily sensation on which that satisfaction rests. Therefore it cannot be counted a loss. Likewise with all the pleasures.

To have never been born – allowing that that is a projection of those who were born speculating on alternatives and probably not a thing in itself – would mean avoiding all the pains and sorrows that inevitably come with life. But avoiding pain must count as a good thing, be it physical pain, or emotionally or psychologically derived. Even death, if that is counted an ill, is avoided. Threat or possibility of hell and damnation are avoided. God does not, presumably, send the never conceived to hell.

The only question about death worth asking is whether it can be worse than life. If not, then why worry? If so, then how? Life never ends. I will forever be a bicycle riding, prescription drug-taking, jobless, unhappy, angry, solitary, God-blessed (I don't believe in God) empty man. Nothing will ever change. I will never change, not for a million years or ten million or eternity.

So when Leticia is found raped and strangled and dumped in the field behind her house I know suspicion will fall on me – sometimes, perhaps, I suspect myself. But who suffers from it more than I? Who is more chilled, more devastated, more unnerved or distraught? Leticia was everything I was not. She was young, a girl: intelligent, open, thoughtful, friendly, full of potential. Full of, well, love maybe.

I am interviewed by the police but point out that it is a small town and everyone knows everyone else, and everyone knew Leticia. There is really no reason to choose me instead of another. They had to agree with me. No one saw me. I do not mention the other friend she talked about. Why would I? *I* was Leticia's friend. There is no one in the open field. There is no one on my list. I was not there. I did not see. I cannot help…I can help.

I decide there is only one way to make it right, only one thing to do. I will be Leticia's killer. From now on I killed her. I will take possession of the tragedy. I will take ownership of life's guilt. I will play the game. I will lose. And that will mean I will win.

❋

Leticia had sat beside me on the curb.

"Next week is your birthday, no?"

"Yes," I said.

"You should have a birthday present. I will make you something."

"You don't have to do that," I said, thinking, a birthday present – when was the last time I had a birthday present?

"Anyway," she said, and that settled that.

Four

Everything, it seems, stems from desire. Our bodies hunger – we desire to not hunger, we get hungrier, we desire more desperately to not hunger. We realize, being thinking, experiential beings, that some things we can do will move us closer to our desire, say, making a sandwich, and some things we may do will not move us closer to our desire, say, putting wet newspapers on our head.

If we internalize this pattern, that some behaviours advance us to our goal, and some do not, that is, that if we want to not be hungry it is good to eat food, and that if we want to not be hungry it is not good to not eat food, we are using the word 'good' to mean effective.

A good (effective) way to make a profit is to reduce costs. A good (effective) way to reduce costs is to use cheap labour. A good way to get cheap labour is to use slavery. Therefore a good way to make money is to use slaves. And making money is a good (effective) way to buy luxuries. And buying luxuries is a good (effective) way to...make me happy, which is a good way to...keep my will to live strong, and keeping my will to live strong is a good, effective way to...? The questions formulated that way are endless until we stop them by saying, "It is just *good*." The Good is where we stop asking for justification.

I stand watching Carole and Jessica play a running game in the square – a two-person game of tag. Carole's long sleek, dark hair is her most striking feature, but I remember her best for her prayers for my mother. I will make certain nothing untoward happens to my Carole. Jessica is blonde and plump.

I see the newspaper vendor go by. I see the nut seller and his cart. I see the bus pull up twice. I see two nuns. I see teenagers, businessmen, shoppers, air takers, and Simon the police officer go by. Some loiter a little, or a lot; some hurry by. Some I see go up the avenue, and then a half-hour later come back down the avenue. I see Robert setting up to take photographs of the new flowers in the median of the street. And more importantly, all those people see me.

I take out a paper bag from my pocket – it crinkles like I am walking on leaves barefoot down the alley to find the dog sniffing at the neighbour's garage again. The sweets stick together in a largish lump of hard candy, as they often do when they are kept in my pocket and the heat sweats them – they are sold unwrapped, no individual, separate, unwaxed paper wrappers like in the capital – and I hit the bag against the lamppost. By rolling the bag in my fingers I can tell the candy has broken loose from itself. One hand in my pocket, the other supporting the open bag on the bottom and holding it out, I step down and whistle a bit. "*Petite chérie*," I say. Carole instantly stops and looks at me, and Jessica, farther away, stops and looks at Carole. I jiggle the bag a little.

"Go ahead," I say.

Carole reaches in and takes a hard red and white striped candy – it might even be two stuck together – and looks at it. I hold the bag out to Jessica. Emboldened by her playmate taking one, Jessica reaches in and takes one too.

Carole waits until they both have one in their hands before she puts hers in her mouth and Jessica follows. I take one myself and pop it dramatically into my mouth with two fingers, smile a big grin, bounce my eyebrows, ruffle Carole's hair and saunter off.

✵

Of course, say philosophers, if goodness is a means to another end, if the end changes, the 'goodness' changes. If the end is the laughter and the peace of immortal death then knives become good tools of Great Goodness. No?

Riding my bicycle past the yellow soy fields to the cemetery by Vanier's farm I realize I probably have a slow leak in my rear tire. I stop, get off, take out my patch and repair kit and wish for a stream or a tub of water. I know there is a ditch a little farther on, but it is often dry. Still, I walk my bicycle along the stones of the road and the dust and do not mind, do not care, see nothing wrong with the sun or the manure or the turkey vultures or the climb uphill and the sweat on my forehead and under my arms. It is the body that unites us to the world. It is our sense of smell, of touch, the impress of the stones on our soles, the sight in our eyes of the horizon of small trees to the north beyond the corn field, the body wet with rain or chill from the nippy air in winter, or the roughness of tree trunk against your shoulder blades, eating your cheese and lettuce by the roadside next to your disabled bicycle – the impression of the seat of which is still between your buttocks.

And peeing into the bushes and proceeding on my way and finding dark green, fishless, thick water welling up in spots in the ditch, known as Lenin Drain. I trundle down the side to immerse – not myself, not baptism – but my deflating, weight-bearing, universally circular rubberized (they make condoms out of rubber) back rear bicycle tube up to my ankles. I bend over looking for the escape of tiny bubbles to indicate the tire's breath.

The point of going to the graveyard by Vanier's farm is to see Laura Ferndale. Laura is the closest thing to courting I am doing, or have long done. She is my age, heavy-ish, but not ridiculously so, and with eyes as warm as sunflowers at noon. I hold her hand and the scent from it is like popovers and sweet, sweet teas and cinnamon and love. She always smells like love, all over, every plane and crevice, her hair and breath, her lengths and curves. I am calling on her to tell her it is over between us. I have moved on. There are other dreams, other places I must go, things I must be. I have put her behind me. The future is always the same, only the past can be changed. People think the past is dead. I hear them say it all the time, but I don't believe it. I think the past is alive. I think if anything, it is the present that is fixed and the past that changes. There is only one way for the present to be and it is. It is the past that we are constantly adding to. It is the past that is constantly changing and it is the past that thrives and grows larger and closer, till it is the past that overtakes and consumes us. It is only in being consumed that we have hope. We all know that.

Goodness, of course, would be most valuable if it was an end in itself. That's obvious. So our task is to establish *in* everyone a desire to be good, *with* everyone a correct understanding of what the good is, and to facilitate *for* everyone the achieving of goodness. The end of 'the Good' is the production of goodness and the Good produces goodness by being known. And so on, and so on, ad infinitum.

Ah! Something stings me under the eye, or bites, and I squeeze it shut and brush my cheek with my thumb. Tears well up and I imagine it swelling and red. Perhaps I will be unable to see for a day or so, or it will turn black like I've been in a fight. My eye begins to throb, each pulse of blood into my head hurts like a twist around my throat. I peddle on, crying.

It occurs to me I cannot really go to see Laura like this. Red and teary eyed, pained, stuttering, sweating from the ride, dirty from dust, notifying her in my way that I am putting an end to our time together. She deserves to see me at my best.

That being the case, I am already there. I can see her standing along the wire and post fence in the long grass beside the walnut. I hesitate in my mind. I often hesitate in my mind. I go up to her.

If I were the only life in existence, would I recognize or feel a difference between Good and Evil? If not, what would my motivations be? Pleasure and pain; interest and boredom? 'Good' would either mean pleasure or it would mean nothing. If I suddenly discover a second life form, how or why does anything change? What has this new life form added? I am still the same entity I was.

Lying, or rather sitting up, on the matted grass beside Laura, I button up my pants and consider the situation I am in.

If I bang my finger I feel pain, and I have a location for the pain – the finger I banged. The pain may actually be being perceived in my head, but I still locate the pain in my finger – a physical location.

If a woman breaks my heart I have emotional pain – it feels undeniably pain-like, save that there is no physical place I can locate it. I don't have a pain in my elbow or toe, but I have a pain. As someone clinically depressed I know that emotional or psychological pain can bring devastation and that *pain* is what it is – but *where* is it? If it is in my brain why can't my brain refer it there the way it refers it to my finger? And what exactly has received the injury? Has my brain been 'hurt'? How? Not materially. By a perception? Of what? A feeling? Doesn't the brain create feeling? Why can a physical event like the sight of a woman walking away from you produce, force, your brain to respond with a non-physically locatable but physically real pain?

But, of course, Laura is not saying goodbye. I am saying goodbye. But I discover a truth, that my leaving her entails her leaving me, my saying goodbye entails her saying goodbye. My breaking up with her involves our breaking up with each other, together, on each side. As much as I do not want, I want. As much as I am determined, I second-guess. As much as I am relieved, as much as I want relief from Laura, from us, from me, I want the familiar, the reassuring. I want to sail but I want to keep the shore I have left in sight. What I do not want is the open, vast, borderless sea. But a sinking boat carries no passengers. Whatever that means.

Laura is very quiet, pulling apart blades of grass, looking into her own lap. There is no good way to live. There is no good way to be human. It involves killing and cruelty and selfishness and hurt and aging and consumption and funerals. Mama weighed eighty pounds when she went and had bald spots on her head. If she were the dog, I would have said it was mange.

Laura's breasts are full and large, but breasts are mainly fat, unlike penises, which are blood. There is something significant in that fact, I am sure. There is something significant in every fact.

So, I decide, what the world is, what life is, is the sum total of all actual facts, physical, biological, chemical, historical, genetic, cosmological – religious? – evolutionary. If you had a piece of paper long enough you could list every fact of the world and you, when you were done, would have achieved the end and purpose of being human, which is the successful cataloguing of the world's rules.

We must keep in mind that there is a distinction between the natural and the supernatural. The natural is what is known, and it is real. The supernatural is what we can't know, and it is not real. Of course, if God exists, you could argue he is natural – in the old sense of naturally occurring, not made out of plastics or tinfoil or the transistors they used to put in radios – is natural in that he is not person-made. But whether God does or does not exist is irrelevant. It does not make life any more or less hard, any more or less easy, or pleasant or bad. God does not – the bastard – make life any more meaningful because there is no explanation for God. God just is. The universe just is. I just am. Leticia, Mama, Jerome St. Monere, whose stone we recline near and who had died in 1837, just were. And are not now. So life goes and so we go through life, shown love sort of the way a magician shows a magic trick, turning nothing into something as a surprise, and then as a double surprise turning it back into nothing again.

So I stay there until finally Laura gets up and leaves and I relax, lying back and looking at the white whispers of cloud in the sky, the blue ocean of sky, borderless it seems, and calm, reassuring.

"Life is good," I think. I am sure Jerome St. Monere misses it, wherever he is now. I always think of the dead as knowing they are dead, as existing and not existing at the same time. I think there is something Buddhist in that, I'm not sure. All religion is bunk. People die.

So, Laura has been removed from my life, or I from hers. I dust myself off and begin back again the way I have come, having first a drink from my thermos of tea. Tea is a concession to an earlier age. I do not drink coffee. It is always tea...the Queen would be proud of me, and what more do we want than that the people we love (I do not love the Queen) be proud of us?

Five

Leticia's funeral is on a Monday at the Catholic church – there is only one Catholic church in town, and another farther out in the county. But I stand outside and follow apart from the crowd, like a boy at a dance but not really part of the dance, hanging awkwardly about a corner or against a wall, wanting to leave and yet wanting to be there. I am sure everyone saw me.

So if I didn't kill Leticia, and I don't think I did, who did kill her? No doubt her uncle, or one of his friends. Perhaps one of her friends, or the janitor at her school, or one of the so-far respectable men of the town: the mayor, or a doctor, or the editor, with some secret vice, turned in by his wife unable to tolerate it anymore, a scandal, a cause celeb no one could fathom. We were waiting for that to happen.

What did happen is that life went on and forty thousand more children died in the world of preventable diseases every day for the next four days, and no one in our town mourned them, or saved them, or knew: except me. What is the cure for death? Death. Guilt. Sorrow. Death. Hell. Punishment. Love. Writing?

When my disability payment comes I put fifty cents in a can on my bedroom dresser. When I have enough I will sponsor a child in Africa. That poor, ignorant black baby, starving, sick, abandoned, with no games to play, no mother's love, no friends, no pets – a blank slate, a person-void, a child-shaped hole I will fill in. Charity, they say, begins at home, but charity, I say, that stays at home isn't charity. Faith and hope....

There is a large dog that often comes into my yard, threatening my smaller dog. It is a beefy black and brown affair, with a square nose and short ears and a bobbed tail. I can see it urinating against a maple by the fence. Guy is asleep on the couch, but he seems to know the stranger is there. He lifts his head, his ears prick up; alert. Guy is a brave dog. He would fight the larger animal and he would die. Guy does not understand the value of discretion and cowardice.

The other dog sniffs his own urine, and, satisfied that it is acceptable urine, up to his normal standards of urine and not that cheap inferior store-bought urine people serve you nowadays and try to pass off as their own baking, trots around the corner of the house and out of sight. Peeing in public and proud of it. It is a dog's life.

I used to have a cat but I convinced John to take her because I caught her scratching the furniture one day. The furniture is important. I want everything to be the same as it was, has always been, around me. I want stability, memory, respect. I want nothing to change. Except life, perhaps. *Le plus ça change....*

So I am older now, by, what, seconds – I have a whole new perspective on life than when I last inhaled. Time does that. The brain ages. Dementia, senility, tiredness, forgetfulness, aches and pains. My mother wore a cloth diaper the last six months of her life and it was necessary that I change it for her and wash it out and apply it, which I did. We have no place to put old people in our town and I'd no money to place anyone there anyway. And all it made me think of was who will look after me when I am her age.

She was buried not in Vanier's Cemetery, but in Green Mountain, called Green Mountain for some reason no one knows; there certainly are no mountains around our town. Not for a long way, and there they mine and cut lumber and make paper and it is hardly a place, in those Canadian mountains, you would call 'Green' or bury someone or think of your eternal rest. But that's what they call it.

The ceremony had been a small affair. Ralphie, the butcher, had come in his best black clothes with his best pomade in his hair and took off his white apron at the graveside and lowered his head. Robert was there, but Robert goes to everyone's funeral, not casually, but seriously. It is a service, mourning, he provides his fellow man, and very Christian of him it is too. The priest, or priest-like-person, the non-denominational Reverend Walters, Rebecca Walters, is actually United, but described her services as non-denominational – and perhaps they were, what do I know? – but was still thought of as 'that United woman.'

There were seven of us there: me, Rebecca, Ralphie, Robert, John, Genevieve Bockman (a friend of mother's) and Mrs. Bluto, our, and still my, neighbour – it was her garage Guy was always trying to get into. So we mourned, more or less, depending, and we buried her and we walked away and everything seemed so...odd, so very, very odd. That is what I remember, what I felt; it was a very odd thing to be doing, to have happen. My mother had never died before and my father, well, if he was dead we had not heard of it. And one day they will do it for me, but what that is I do not know.

The doors are open – it could be anything. Death, whatever it was, *might* be anything. No one knows. Yet, oddly, everyone thinks they know. Christians, Jews, Muslims, doctors, atheists, everyone has their scenario they tell themselves, but no one *knows*. It could be anything at all. It is almost *exciting*.

I make toast, as I always do before bed and eat it with a little jam, just a little jam, but no butter. Butter is an expense, and unnecessary – I am going to put jam on it anyway, why do I need to put butter on it first? The jam is from Mrs. Bluto's preserves, seedy and tart.

Tomorrow I must do it. It has waited a long time, patiently, for me to do it, and tomorrow I will. But I say that every night. I lick the jam knife, first running it along my tongue, then pulling it between my lips, teeth apart and making a smacking sound. The sound amuses me, like a sloppy kiss, a playful bottom-slap, a muffled fart or a high-five. Finishing, I brush my teeth and go to bed.

Every night, some time in the night, Guy gets onto the bed with me. He is never there when I go to sleep; he is always there when I wake up. It has been like this his whole life. I never notice him; I always find him.

This time Guy wakes me up. He is barking early in the morning. It is still dark. The middle of the night. He never does that. I am tired, muddle-headed, and angry. I do not get out of bed. There is much ado outside, I can hear it now, the bell of the ambulance – or is it a police car? – rings clearly.

I close my eyes, exhale, and get up. I put on my robe and go to the window. I can see shapes. I can hear what I assume are voices but cannot understand or make out words. I scratch Guy's ears, put the lead on him and go outside.

It is Mrs. Bluto's house. And it is an ambulance, not a police car. And firetrucks. The firetrucks come to put out the fire. But then that is what firetrucks are for. They fail. The fire smoulders to a finish, having consumed everything that was once there. But you can still tell it was a house.

"*Qui est-ce?*" I say to Robert.

"Pardon?" he says.

"Oh. How is she?" I say.

"She is dead, I believe. They have put her in there," and he indicates the hospital van.

"How did it happen?"

"You knew her."

"Yes."

"You were her friend."

"Yes."

"She was old."

"Yes."

"Still..."

"Yes," I say, "still..."

Robert does not live in the neighbourhood. Why is he here? How is he here? It is two in the morning. Is he just passing by? But Robert is more insomniac than murderer, I'd bet. Still, one wonders. I am not sure Mrs. Bluto is dead. It is not something I can be sure of – people dying. It is hard to know what that is. Mrs. Bluto was younger than my mother, a widow since the wreck on *The Roland Barts* twenty years ago: the death of the sailor.

I still have a pantry of her preserves and eat one of her pickles every morning for the protein. I have become health conscious. I always eat lots of vegetables because they are generally cheaper than meat and less off-putting to prepare. I drink cow's milk fresh from the dairy and I drink plenty of water to flush my system out. I wear a hat in the sun. I do not eat butter. I do deep knee bends and sit-ups. I do not go outside on smog days.

Still, I feel my age, especially when I look at the young girls of school age and, since I still think of myself as in high school, still fill my fantasies with me as I am now, there among the people and females of my high school time, they as pretty and desirable as they were at seventeen, me much cooler and smarter and funnier than I ever was at seventeen, but there, sitting across the desk from Shelley Tenner or Daphne Husene or Ella Agnew, shining. I think men's magazines and men's longings find their way to the topic of teenage school girls because that is usually our first sexual thought or memory, the first, at least for my generation, we noticed. It is the world we were young in, and no matter how old we get, we always, I believe, think of ourselves as seventeen.

Six

Suicide, I remind myself, is immoral in most religions because it usurps God's prerogative to choose my death himself. It is illegal because it is murder. In both cases, the argument is that I do not have sufficient rights over my own life to be allowed to end it. However, if I were to sacrifice my life to save someone else – that would be moral and legal. I have enough rights over my own life to do that, but not to put myself out of intractable physical pain no one else can feel or to end pedophiliac or violent tendencies (never acted on) that torment but which no one else knows about.

If it is a question of rights, I have the right to kill someone in self defence, or stand there meekly and let them kill me, and the government has the right to kill me if I am convicted (rightly or wrongly) of what it considers a capital offence (blasphemy or murder), and foreign governments have the right to kill me in wartime and I'm just collateral damage. If I faint and fall in front of an oncoming train, no one is under any legal or moral obligation to risk their own life to pick me up; if, however, they manage to film my death they can sell the footage to the news and make money. If I have cancer no one can force me to take treatment.

As far as religions go, a religion, or more admittedly, a cult, recently committed mass suicide because they thought a space ship would take them to Mars if they did. Religious reasons are binding on those of that religion and therefore to prove them you would have to prove the religion itself, which few can do. Suffice it to say everyone has the right to end their own life but not mine. This is not a recommendation. Anyone who feels suicidal should seek help. Talk to a priest. I was suicidal for ten years – I may still be suicidal – but I got help from Guy. Suicide is a tragedy, and given how little we know about death, no guarantee of solving the problem. But it is not immoral if morality is regarded as a matter of rights, what you have the right to do and what you do not. This makes it seem like Freedom.

I watch Jackie walk down the street. I am sitting outside the post office. It is an official government building. Jackie is an artist, with an artist's studio. That is not all she is, of course. No one can afford to be just an artist. Not even in a small town. Her hope is that we can become a tourist place, a place tourists will come to see us and our quaint ways. So she can sell her weavings and her drawings. She thinks we have potential. We do not have potential. Potential left town long ago. It is an insult to be quaint. It is one step away from being eccentric, and being eccentric means to fight loneliness with something other than people, with habits and thoughts and games and ideas and animals and windmills and causes and routines of excruciating art or beauty.

It is not right; it is not *right.* I can only save so many. My life raft is only so big. I can only pull so many out of the water. The water: not waving, drowning. Someone has painted, in English, NUKE THE WHALES, on the alley-side of her studio.

Every one knows what Jackie and Gerald are cooking up. Politics.

❋

When I was in the mountains on a walking tour once I stayed in a hut/inn where we had potatoes and bacon for breakfast. There were two other hikers staying there, a couple, male (tall and blond) and female (slim and dark), who billed and cooed the whole time. I even caught a glimpse, well, a look, at the woman showering through a chink in the wooden wall. Her legs were extraordinarily thin for a nature walker, toothpick like, and she did not shave her underarms or bikini area. Her buttocks and breasts were small, but her hair was long and glorious, shiny and sleek and lathered up, rolled and caressed and squeezed out, and she combed it, scratching herself between her legs before towelling off and dressing.

By the time she came out I was putting on my boots on the other side of the yard, with my gear on my back and my head down. I walked for six hours that day and rested by a lakeside and smelled pine and bear dung and dead fish. I relaxed and thought about nature and the world, and my youth, and my father who left when I was twelve but used to take me to the fairs and tractor pulls and Art in the Park and the Tomato Festival and walks for cancer and to see horses at his friend's place and then said good-bye after something happened – I never found out what. I thought of Emily, the naked hiker, and her body, exposed and absolute, open to me and my eye, my brain, in my memory. I did not wish to make love to her, to enter, to fuck her. I wished only to look at her, think about her, study her, be present, until I understood what it is I do not understand, what no one understands. Until I could put my finger on that truth I can never quite put my finger on.

Sometimes – some people – and I think maybe, maybe…but people die, or hide from you inside their houses, or go off into the mountains with their boyfriends. Everything escapes you eventually, even the things you never had, even the people. Females.

I have not been in the mountains for a long time. Times are tougher there now; lumber tariffs, low commodity prices, stronger pollution laws, protestors, all contribute. Plus, I am perhaps more lonely now, less seeking out solitude and stoic, silent, grand nature. Small town life, dogs and gardens and children, people and small shops, the once a week newspaper, the creeks and farms and restaurants (three) that all hang about each other, and about me, or me about them, in the small town life of a small town. And the town is getting smaller. The bank's head office is closing our branch. It is the only financial institution we have. We will have to go forty minutes east to get to another bank. There is talk of getting a Credit Union, but there's not much you can do. There's not much you can do to change the universal laws of personality or fate or the age you are born into, or capitalism, or justice, or desire.

❋

I think about using the telephone and consider that it is probably tapped. Nevertheless I call Carole's parents.

"There was a strange man watching Carole in the street. He stood there and watched her. Did Carole tell you?"

"No."

"I think you should ask her. With what's going on…"

"Yes, yes, I will."

People say that children are the future; I hear it all the time. It is what you call a 'cliché'. But really, don't they mean that adults are what is important and that children are significant, not as children, but as future adults? Children are not important, not as children. They are investments in adulthood, with either positive or negative returns. The Prime Minister will never be a ten-year-old, but a ten-year-old might be Prime Minister one day. We do not get younger as time goes on, closer to our birth, we get farther from it, less childlike. Childhood is not the future: old age, senility, death, war, those are the future. Childhood, if you are a child (I am a child of God, alas) is *now*.

Nevertheless it is important to treat children well because if you don't they will punish you in your old age. Life is about punishment. Religion is about life and it is about punishing the innocent. All those martyrs marching gloriously, enthusiastically to their deaths. Jesus arranging his own execution – or God arranging it. Peter crucified – a good man, a fisherman – upside down. All of us sinners because of Adam, because of what some stupid, half-educated, pussy-whipped man did – not me – generations and generations before I was born. And I am guilty. Guilty of being human. Guilty of being me. Guilty of being alive.

And guilt, guilt calls for sacrifice. Either forced – we put you in jail, we fine you, we hang you – or voluntary, alms to the poor, confession, self-flagellation, neurosis, abstinence, suicide, murder.

The people who feel no guilt we call sociopaths and fear. The people who overcome guilt we call saints, convinced God loves them and heals them. The people who feel 'appropriate' guilt we call well-adjusted. The people who do not know what to do with their guilt we call artists, and the person, the man, who seeks guilt out and is not guilty we call the messiah. I have no mission in life. I am neither one thing nor the other, neither alive nor dead, neither guilty nor innocent.

Chesterton – do you know Chesterton? – He was an English author – said something like (I paraphrase) that when a regular person is faced with two truths that contradict each other – guilt and innocence, say – he (or she) will take both truths and live with the contradiction. What a charmer he was. To recognize that truths can contradict each other, to point out that it is the living that is important, not the contradiction. To exist and not exist, both – there is hope.

❋

John is telling me that Gerald, who works at the bank, is being transferred. I asked what that means for Jackie.

John shrugs. "He is our most eligible bachelor," he says, "Now, if I had his money…"

"She will not go," I say. "She will not go. Her life is here. She will find someone else."

"It might be love."

"There is more than just love of a person. There is love of self, there is love of place."

"It is good money."

"There is no such thing as good money."

"So you, Pierre, eh? How are you? You have your eye on our Jackie?"

There is a whole world out there, I think.

"The Americans are at war," I say.

"The Americans are always at war. They are a proud people. There is not a poverty-stricken third world country anywhere in the world that can stand up to the might of America's fighting men and women. They have proven that many times."

What would it be like to be an American, I wonder. It must be neurotic. To believe Israel is always right but that all the Jews in the world are going to burn in hell for eternity for not being Christians. To believe in democracy at home but overthrow democracies abroad. To claim to be the land of opportunity, but seek to keep the poorest immigrants – the illegals – out. But then Americans are the richest, best-looking, sexiest, most powerful people on earth. Everyone in the world wants to sleep with an American.

The fire that burnt Mrs. Bluto's house spared her garage and when they opened it they found rabbits there, which they let out of their cages and which ran away. Throughout the following weeks we saw them loping about yards and the golf course over town. My thought was of Australia, where rabbits breed without predators and hundreds of them can move across a farmer's field en masse and eat everything in sight. Perhaps the human hold on the dominant species slot of the earth is not so strong as we'd like to think. Perhaps crowds, hundreds, a thousand, six billion, ravenous, plant destroying, defecating rabbits, instinctively feeding and fucking, moving across the landscape mindlessly is how we look to birds, or coyotes or lynx. It is good to see ourselves as others see us. It is better to have others see us as we see ourselves.

Mrs. Bluto is in the hospital for four weeks with burns. When she comes out, is 'released', she is in a wheelchair and cannot live alone, and, of course, her house is unliveable. So I take her in for one month, while her daughter in the city makes arrangements. She is ugly (Mrs. Bluto, not the daughter), scarred, shiny, red, hairless – she wears an orange wig – fleshy and tiny-eyed, and she is bored, so bored, and frustrated and afraid. We sit and listen to the news at six o'clock every night, me at the kitchen table sitting in my chair and she in the middle of the room sitting in her wheelchair. It is a ritual with me, the evening news, and she will just have to adapt to it.

"*Je ne sais pas*," she says.

"Pardon?"

"There is no fool like an old fool."

We have just heard a story about the Pope praying for the astronauts. "Why do you say that?" I ask.

"It is horrible," she says.

Usually when I sit at the table and do nothing I break off small pieces of bread, very small, pick them off, and roll them on the table under my finger, or between finger and thumb, like something I picked out of my nose. It is a habit I have taken over from my mother, who did it while drinking her evening tea all her life, or all of her life that I could remember. It irritates Mrs. Bluto.

"Must you, must you, must you? Eh?" she says. "It is a filthy habit."

I stop. It is neither a good thing nor a bad thing. It is just a thing, just what I do. Still, for her sake I put an end to it, and just drum my fingers lightly, fingertips, pads only, on the table.

"I cannot stand that noise," she says to me. "You know you are an irritating person, Pierre. You know that about yourself, don't you? What your mother must have gone through, poor woman. And a widow."

By 'widow' Mrs. Bluto meant simply 'with no man around' – mother never said anything about father being dead, and she would have told me. She would certainly have been sure to have definitely told me if he had, if she had known. There's no doubting that.

"I want to go outside," Mrs. Bluto says. She is a gardener, or had been, all sorts of flowers and plants, roses and tulips and daffodils and I don't know, different sizes and shapes, leaves of plants all in her big back garden and all along the front walk to her door – now consumed in ashes forever. Compost, if you think of it that way.

"You'll need a hat," I say.

"I have one. On the sideboard."

I go and get it. She puts it on her head. "If I cannot live in my garden I can at least look at it," she says.

"There is my garden."

"Ha. Grass and maples and spruce. That's not a garden. Still, you are a man, it is different for you." I thank her for that recognition.

"Now," she says, "I want to go now, please."

So I wheel her out, with difficulty down the steps, but she does not seem to mind, to a shady spot that I can see from the window, and go back inside. I cannot spend all my time with her, nor do I think she wants me to. Even she must want to be alone a little, as frightening as that must be in some ways. Guy is inside with me.

"Do not doubt," the priest had said, "that there is life."

Seven

A person should always consider the value of non sequiturs. A non sequitur is something that does not follow from what went before (I think it is Latin, or one of those dead things). I can actually worry myself into being unable to sleep or into feeling miserable about myself or the world over issues such as the world hunger problem, or how to construct an argument you can make to politicians to be able to avoid and refuse all wars forever, or people's inhumanity to each other or how was the Holocaust possible. And what appears to me now to be the apparent answer to all those questions and issues is to have a family, maybe a pet, take a vacation in the summer, read a good book, and spend time with people you like. That is everyone's response, and I'm not even saying it is wrong or people should be ashamed or refute it; I am just now discovering that it works.

If I say millions of people are starving in the world, the correct response seems to be that my favourite show is on television tonight. *How* does this work? How can reading a good book answer the question of the value of my life given my certain death or the genocide in Rwanda? Is it simply distraction? I don't think so. I think that somehow small personal satisfactions answer our need for value, meaning and point to life more than, or at least, as much as, philosophical schemes do. What does this mean? What does it say about us? It says that as long as we are not in pain, physical or psychological, we do not much care about much else. The remarkable people are the people who *are* in pain over the world's hunger problem, or wars, or homelessness in Winnipeg. And those are not many.

For most of us, the pain in our lives is caused not by genocide in Africa (unless you are African) but by loneliness in our life, or boredom in our life, or a lack of some material good, or by pain in the lives of those we love, or by frustration at work, or in sex. Were it to be the other way around, and our pain was caused by the state of the world's poor more than by sexual frustration or lack of a good car in our own lives, well then, wouldn't we *all* be Mother Teresa?

Down at the beach tonight it is deserted save someone has built a campfire. I can see two outlined shapes sitting side-by-side facing the flickers. Lovers, I imagine. Perhaps teenagers, though teenagers don't do that sort of thing much. With them it is all dancing and driving and drinking pop outside the late night Variety. Perhaps they are romantic, cultured teenagers, the kind that hold promise for our future. I wait until I am behind them and I say, "What are you doing?"

They turn around. It is Jackie and Gerald. They look distraught.

Jackie worries about the bomb. I'm sorry, but who worries about the bomb these days? Gerald is younger than Jackie. He does not worry about the bomb. Jackie needs to be more like Gerald. I think they both know it. I know what Jackie is doing. She is remaking Jackie.

The bomb. There is something romantic about suicide pacts. Everyone going together in a war – it is stupid to protest the bomb. It is stupid to protest the weapons of war. The weapons of war are not the problem. War is the problem. I think she is a spy.

To not believe in the Atom Bomb is to not believe in Israel and America, who have Atom Bombs, or French culture or cuisine because the French have them, or British literature since they have it. And how can we give all those things up?

No, I am a sentimentalist, and there is something beautiful in total destruction. There is something profound in extinction. So sue me. It is the way of the world.

"God, Pierre," Jackie says, "what do you want? How long have you been standing there?"

"You shouldn't sneak up on people." Gerald says.

"What do you want?" I ask.

"Nothing, Pierre, we're fine…" Jackie says, "Gerald…"

"Do you always walk around at night?" Gerald says.

"Yes," I say, "I make my rounds."

"Really?" Gerald seems to be considering this. "Do you ever go down by Turkey Creek?"

"No," I say, "I am afraid of turkeys." This is a joke, satire, because no one in my lifetime has ever seen a turkey at Turkey Creek. None of us really know why it has that name. Settlers two hundred years ago. Once a thing gets labelled it is impossible to change.

"What do you want?" I ask again.

"Nothing, I want for nothing, Pierre, I'm just..."

"Pierre, listen to me," says Gerald. "You should go home. You should not be out walking around at night. People will talk."

"You should stay," I say to Gerald. "You should stay with Jackie. You shouldn't go. She is a fine woman. The town needs you two."

"That's fine, Pierre."

"The water is very cold," I say. I have not been in the water, but I know it is cold because it goes without saying. It is water; it is always cold.

"Perhaps you would like to swim?" I suggest. Jackie, however, is dressed, pulls the blanket closer around her.

"I'm going to have to ask you to leave," Gerald says, "okay?"

"I'm sorry. I was just out. I didn't know you. I thought you were young people."

Jackie laughs at that. "Well, we're not that old! But Gerald's right. Go home to Guy. We were just talking. I'll see you tomorrow at the fair."

She is right. The fair is tomorrow. I should be sleeping so I can be early. Community fairs are, well, I imagine they are the same everywhere there are small communities. There will be hot dogs and corn on the cob, balloon-tying barkers, candy, young men in muscle shirts, small girls in cut-offs, lots of sunglasses. Tractors.

"Good night," I say finally, and climb up the incline to the town street. One year they had a kissing booth with Miss Milk in it but I did not do anything. I do not like the idea of people knowing how I kiss. I seldom kissed Laura, not on the lips; pecks on the cheek, nibbles on the ear or neck, cunnilingus, but not kissing. Most people breathe through their mouth so kissing is a kind of suffocation. It is control. It is, in its own way, an act of violence. Besides, it is unsanitary. Miss Milk was twenty-four.

There is a car moving slowly ahead of me and I see someone throw something out the passenger window as it speeds off. When I get there I see what it is. A beer bottle – Budweiser – smashed against the sidewalk. I have been finding beer bottles under the tall spruce in my front yard, the one by the road, and I guessed it was someone, kids, parking and drinking. I scuff as much of the broken glass into a pile as I can with my shoe and walk on. There are probably wolves out tonight, I think to myself. I must hurry home.

There is not much a person can do about the body they inherit. Tall or skinny, or alcoholic, or what you like or don't, this food or that, these people or those, how nervous you are. How smart your brain is.

Everything is physical. All our thoughts, dreams, fears, desires, loves, hunger, knowledge, all chemicals and electricity in the brain. The mind is an illusion. It is an irony that the physical world can give rise to the illusion of a non-physical world. I bite my fingernails, hard – that is as much who I am, that is more who I am than who or what I love. If Miss Milk is there I will slap her face.

She is not there. Instead it is a young man, anonymous, blond, freckled, in his twenties. This strikes me as perverse. To encourage homosexuality at a town fair, where children, girls, mothers are. But I am fascinated and watch the kissing booth. There is not much activity. I see two teenage girls go up in thirty minutes. They will not make any money. Someone has miscalculated. I feel sorry for the boy. Girls apparently do not like kissing. I can smell salt.

Salt and butter on popcorn. Ring toss. Air rifles and targets. Prize pigs. Lots of suntans. Babies on shoulders. Cotton candy. Hand-holders. Stuffed Snoopy dogs. Hats. It is a horrible, horrible day. After I have been there an hour or less I want to kill myself. How can any of this be? People's ignorance is an insult to my unhappiness.

But, I calm down. I relax. I should have brought Guy, walked him around on a leash. He would have liked that – the smells, the sounds, the people. There are even a few other dogs being taken about. Guy likes that sort of thing. Dogs need stimulation and I know I have not been good for Guy. Still, all these people are here, and everyone has forgotten.

It is an on-going conundrum. To be truly hopeless is to realize that there is no hope even in death or suicide or courage or pessimism, in nihilism or insanity, in acting or not acting, in living or not. This is because the problem is always one of how we respond to finding ourselves here, alive, in this world. What is the correct response, that is it. And I know it, I know it, have always known it, but no one else does. It is an insight. The correct response is simply to blink.

I am sitting on one of those cement abutments that outline the parking lot so cars don't drive on the grass, and I eat my lunch. A couple pushing a baby stroller comes and stands nearby. The man kisses the woman and goes over to the crowd and lines up. Probably for food.

Then the woman puts the brakes on the stroller and goes over to join him. The baby is sleeping. I am, of course, appalled that two adults would leave a baby unattended next to a stranger in a crowded public place while they both go away, even if it is to buy corn on the cob.

The baby begins to fuss. I look at it, all bundled and fat. It begins to cry. I do not know if I should coochy-coo it under the chin, or talk to it, or rock it back and forth. It is crying and making fists. Perhaps it is its first inchoate realization that it will be abandoned.

I decide to ignore it. When someone you know, when someone you love, is unhappy, has lost someone, has a difficult home life, there is really no sympathy. Everything presents itself as a problem to be solved. What should you say, what is really the problem? There is never any real sympathy, because it is illegal to hug them, hold them, squeeze them, kiss them, stroke them, which is what you would do if you really felt something, if you *really* felt. What do *I* feel? I stand up. I bend and look at, smell, the baby. It is fresh like wheat fields and sunshine, picnics under oak or walnut trees, a new library book. It screams louder. The damn thing doesn't shut up. No one is really perfect. There's something in Darwin about survival of the perfect. Or is it the Bible? I reach out my hand, slowly, right for....

"Excuse me?" a man says. "Are you the father?" He is in uniform. At this point the mother makes some incoherent panicked sound and there is a padding of flip-flops as she hurries over. She is calling for her husband.

"I'd move on if I were you," the uniformed man says – security? No. He is wearing the orange striped vest of someone directing parking. His badge says volunteer. But he is wearing sunglasses and an earpiece. He is dressed in black. He is much bigger than I am.

"It's a baby," I say, "look."

A crowd is in danger of gathering around us. I step back and open my palms. I take another step back. "You have a lovely daughter," I say to the mother. "She was crying."

"It's a boy," she says, moving the carriage.

"Anyway," I say, and turn before someone biblical gets the idea of stoning. It was a baby. I had to look. It was right beside me.

And when tragedy comes, should it come, there is nothing to do.

Eight

What, the priest once asked me, guides our behaviour while we do what we all do, which is wait for death, though he didn't put it that way. The question is always, "What do we do?" or how do we respond to our situation, to what is presented to us, to finding ourselves alive in this world?

What it is to be alive, I think, at least at our stage, is to have experiences (bearing in mind that thoughts are also experiences), and all we do is an attempt to make those experiences, which do not ever add up to anything, add up to something, be it through religion or science or – well, what else is there besides religion and science? We are all just devices, ways, of having experiences, and when we die, as we will, the ones we already have had disappear, are not even memories, cease to be anything, and it is as if we, or our species when it dies, were never here at all.

People think some experiences are of more value than others. The experience of loving a child or a pet is of more value than that of reading a book – or of writing one. People think that if they leave behind art they have painted, or an invention, or wealth to their children, or knowledge they have gleaned or created in their life – Edison left us the light bulb – their lives will have had value because they made a difference in the lives of other people whose lives judged on that same scale do not have value because they invented nothing.

One day there will be no life, no humans. Yes, one day there will surely be nothing, when our species goes extinct, as we must assume it will. No one to read Shakespeare, no one to study particle theory, no one to see the pyramids, no one to fight for the Palestinian or Israeli cause, no one to love anyone, no meaning to the words 'love' or 'justice'. One day, there will be no day.

This is the contract we all signed; this is the vote cast in our name by our parents when they had us. We can embrace nihilism, deny reality, or we can look for loopholes. Look for loopholes. Ultimately, we are all lawyers.

❋

I said I know what Jackie is really like, and what she is really like is Jewish. Our country's government is conservative, which means they are more interested in finding the correct moral stance on a problem than in actually solving it. So their position on the Middle East is that Israel is 100% right and an innocent victim. The rest of us just looked at the mid-east and shook our heads. Why can't they just sit down and resolve their differences like good Christians? Don't they know that in Christ there is no Israeli or Palestinian, no Jew or Muslim, no heterosexual or homosexual – well, there are still heterosexuals and homosexuals, Roman Catholics and Pentecostals, Conservatives and Liberals – but those are distinctions God makes, it is the distinctions man makes that disappear, like slave or free.

Jackie and Gerald. Everyone is so. And Gerald is a good (or not so good – what do I know?) Catholic. I didn't think Jews were allowed to sleep with non-Jews, but maybe she is conflicted or a secret agent. I will not be the one to turn her in. Everyone treats me like I am a little less than I really am. I don't know why I bring out the condescension in people. Harmlessness – that is what I aspire to, being harmless.

I know there are people who hate Jews. I know there are people who hate Protestants. I know there are people who hate immigrants, or children, or dogs, or people on welfare. The problem with the world is that hate always wins. If I love someone and that someone hates me, they win. They can shoot me in the head, strangle me, and I die and then the world belongs to them. The negative is always stronger than the positive. Anti-Semitism is always stronger than tolerance, because the tolerant cannot kill. It is necessary to hate every now and then.

And me, do I, whom do I, hate? I don't hate anyone. I am entirely powerless.

There is a young boy of ten or twelve selling chocolate bars in front of the drug store for some cause. Wheelchair athletes, he says. "Name one," I say, but he cannot. I buy a chocolate bar, overpriced, and of poor quality and keep it. "Sometime today," I think, "I may meet someone who will like a chocolate bar."

I decide to watch the ladies buy dresses through the window of *Chez Louise*. There is a bug crawling on the doorframe, above the door. A caterpillar: yellow and black. I think those are poisonous.

Louise – whose name is Maybelle Bransome – tells me to move along and not stand there. She doesn't want loiterers. So I move along. It is only a bug.

Living is the hardest thing you'll ever do, my old mother used to say, and I must confess to all the times life baffles me. I look around at it: the buildings and trees and people and caterpillars and dogs and I am dumbfounded – what is it all? Why is it here? How is all this possible? What am I supposed to do? I slap myself on the arm and try to squish a mosquito.

I walk on until I come to Lulu tied to a post outside Spunkle's candy and ice cream store. Lulu is a small black and white female dog that belongs to the Lessers. It means one of them is in the store. I bend down and scratch Lulu's head and tell her she is a good dog, until Jessica Lesser and Carole Smart come out of the candy shop.

"Hello, you two," I say. "I was just talking to Lulu. She's a good dog. I can't pass by a dog or cat without wanting to rub its head. Jessica, you will have to bring Lulu over to my place to meet Guy. We can play Monopoly or Junior Scrabble while the dogs make babies. Then you'd have lots of little puppies. You'd like that, wouldn't you, to have a lot of little puppies?"

Jessica is watching Lulu. "I'm not allowed," she says.

"And quite right too," I say, and stand up and ruffle her hair. "You're a special girl," and I move on. Perhaps she will come. Perhaps she will tell her parents. Perhaps Carole will tell. I feel sorry sometimes for Guy, knowing he will never have a girlfriend. It is important to some people.

I write a letter to one of our senators asking for money to be spent to buy mosquito nets for African babies so they don't get malaria and die. It is not easy to be an African baby or the mother of an African baby, getting malaria and dying. So many of them die before the age of five that mothers get used to, know they have to have, a lot of babies just to see a few make it to ten or fifteen or, even fewer, blessed event, to twenty. It must be very hard. I myself am an only child. It is different here.

Once upon a time life first got started – somehow – and those life forms lacked the genes that gave the survival instinct, so they just sat there and did not eat or drink and simply died out. Then, sometime later – somehow – life got started again, and these creatures had the desire to survive and the desire to reproduce, and so evolution was possible and now we have automobiles and satellite radio. But we do not reproduce so that we can evolve; we evolve because we just happen to reproduce. There is no point to reproduction, no goal it moves toward. It is no advantage to any of us here now to have human beings exist three hundred years from now, after we are dead. There is no capital-N nature that has a Way or a Design or a Plan. Life simply is whatever it is and there is no more reason it should not be unpleasant than there is reason it should not be anything else. There is no more reason six-year-olds should not get cancer than there is a reason they should not have blue eyes. There is no such thing as tragedy, there is just life, and life is what it is, whatever it is, and needs no reason, explanation, or argument. The fact is it is stupid to be sad.

The sunsets in our town are beautiful in summer. I would tell you if I knew the names of colours, but I am not a painter. Jacob would know. Leticia's uncle (Leticia is dead, does that make Jacob an ex-uncle?) did landscapes, and sometimes sold one, though I don't think for very much money. Now that I think about it, how did he make his money? It is the first thing you want to know about a person, even before you ask if they are single or not.

"How do you make your money?" people ask, and I say, "With a printing press," and people look puzzled. I should say,

"With an HP laser scanner printer interfacing with digital technology on a Macintosh mainframe." Then people would laugh. I am so behind the times. Technology gives me performance anxiety.

Our job in life, should we choose to accept it, is simply to endure. Not for positive reasons, but for negative. Suicide is wrong. Therefore I am called to endure life, go through it, yes, put up with it, until I die by some means other than my own hand. What is important, what gives pleasure, what makes it bearable, is just that, that I have figured that out about life and if I keep working on it, keep thinking about it, I may figure something else about life out.

⁂

I got to grade twelve in school and found it very hard. I don't mean the work, because I didn't do the work – I didn't study or do homework – I mean everything else. I mean being alive. I understood geography, but I did not understand me. Every day was a life and death struggle with myself, and they wanted me to learn about the bloody Family Compact. They expected me to go to football games – football games! – while I was trying to stop cutting my arms every night with a sharpened kitchen knife before going to bed.

"You sit like a fag," Chas Duguay said to me once because I had crossed my legs at the thigh. Why do people say things to hurt other people? Why cruelty? The need to hurt must be like lust. Always the question: do I fuck or do I kill? I must do one. Roman Catholic priests are all liars. Sex is murder, or murder is sex. I'm sure they must feel the same; feed on the same need. I think that explains serial killers. I have known some liars in my time. I used to be a churchgoer.

❋

It is Tuesday and another child has gone missing. Everyone is talking about it. Who is it? It is a boy this time, taken while at the beach with his young parents. They had taken off all his clothes to let him play in the water. People are strange. We don't say it, but we all know the mother must have been sunbathing topless. We just know.

It was a secluded part of the beach, right near where the trees run up to the water at the point, where there is a log in the shade I like to sit on and eat Hershey's Kisses I bought at the store.

The father keeps saying, "But it happened at the beach. It happened at the *beach*," as if the idea of something bad happening at a beach was somehow incomprehensible to him.

In the morning Guy is sick. It isn't diarrhoea or anything bad like that, just lethargic, off his food, whimpering and hot, I think, probably running a temperature.

What to do with a sick dog? I believe in the body. I believe in the fight that goes on every day inside me between disease and health, bodies and anti-bodies, life and death. Guy will be okay. A little rest, a little time, a little care.

Mrs. Bluto is going to be taken away and I do not expect to ever see her again or hear from or about her again. Her daughter when she comes is a stout woman my age, with dirty blonde hair, who smokes. She goes out alone to the front porch for a cigarette, and Mrs. Bluto cries because she suddenly realizes what her life is. The truth snaps us like kindling for Time's fire, or God's, or Infirmity's. It sets us free by consuming us the way a dog consumes a rabbit, or a man a young boy, or a youth a toddler, and we are never free of it, though we spend our whole lives trying to recover and forget. A truth unrecognized is our only hope; for once we recognize it as a truth, how then can we hope against it?

Sitting in a tree so I can see in Jackie's window, I watch her sit and read, and read, and read, just that. Her hair is in a towel like she has just washed it and she wears a rose-coloured robe. Once when doing this I saw her in her bra. It felt illegal, it felt dirty, but there was no other way I would ever have seen her so. Those who make peaceful change impossible make violent change inevitable. Kennedy said that, and he knew a thing or two about women.

Jackie gets up to talk on the phone with her back to me. There are mosquitoes out and they annoy me. Parasites, they feed off the bodies of others, dashing in for a quick blood bite, and then dashing off again. They do not have the courage or the decency for a face-to-face confrontation, a hand-to-hand battle for life, winner take all. They need you alive so they can suck you again.

I kill a fat one and splatter my own blood against my thigh. Perhaps I will die. The Jains in India believe it is wrong to kill anything, an insect or a bug even. What do they eat, I wonder? If human beings are not special cases, entitled to kill cows and carrots, pigs and potatoes, then the world is a madhouse and we are insane. Everything, our culture, our science, our art, our religion, our families, our politics, our literature, our lives, our dependants, depends on the eaten being less than the eater; if the eaten are equal to or greater than the thing that eats, how can we breathe?

The thing about sex is that I cannot deny it is me; I am feeling the feeling, the pleasure. *I* am feeling the desire, the pressure. *I* am feeling the release. It is like pain. I cannot doubt it is mine and I cannot know someone else's. If I know I exist because I think, I also know I exist because I feel, pleasure or pain, it makes no difference. Though I recommend pleasure, if it can be arranged. It cleanses the body.

Jackie hangs up, and pulls the front of her robe out from her body and looks down at herself, brushing something away. I can sit in a tree a long time. Then she turns the lights out and I think, "One day we will look back on this and laugh. One day perhaps I will turn this into a great painting." Now we see through a glass darkly, but then face to face.

I sit in the tree a long time after the lights are out, out of respect, a kind of cuddling. Then a few quick motions and I am down on the ground and the wet grass, sauntering down Louis toward the school, past the school, to the mechanic's garage, past that to downtown and the cinema showing *Chocolate*, and past three older teenage boys in a group.

"Cur," one says to me.

They heave themselves off the gas station wall.

"Fag," another says.

I look at them. "If we fight," I say, "I may lose, but I will guarantee that one or two of you will be less an eye." I point at them. "You should never fight a crazy man," I say. "You never know what he might do."

They hesitate and I look at them a little longer, then go on my way. They are no threat to me. They are mere children.

I believe, because I am a modern man, that there is meaning in meaninglessness. That random pointless acts of sex or love or violence or consumption or excretion or anger or gentleness or neutralness or war or thinking or walking or looking or – the list goes on, the list includes everything a living thing can or does do – create meaning, real meaning. I believe that ten meaningless things done in a row somehow become meaningful. I believe that a lifetime of individually pointless experiences somehow adds up to meaning and purpose and goodness and satisfaction and worth. I too have given up on meta-narratives. There are only competing fragments, which, when put carefully together over a lifetime, result in a pile of fragments which someone will come along and scatter again with his boot. Tell me there is no beauty in that.

Guy died.

An old man is hit by a car on Rue Street. He was eighty-five years old and the car dragged him fifteen metres before stopping. You can see the smear his body left on the pavement, where the skin was torn off and the red meat and blood of muscle was smushed abstractly, like a painting painted by one of those painters who can't paint.

The trouble with art is that it makes my jaw hurt. It slaps me in the face with the brutal fact of the existence of things not myself. It is so easy, watching TV, reading, looking at my dining room table, sweeping the floor, driving a car (I imagine), even petting the dog, to see it all as in my world, extensions of, connected to, myself. I am the book, I encompass the table, the house, Guy is me, mine, a smaller Siamese twin of me – but Turner, Van Gogh, Munch, Pollock, Bernini, Degas; it is like a woman you love saying no to you. It is like a woman, a child, you love more than God, more than life itself, more than anything that there is, and she says, "I never loved you," "I can't stand you," "Go."

I do not reject art. I never reject art. Art, good art, rejects me. This is because it forces me to acknowledge a reality that is absolutely not-me. Because I have seen Rembrandt I cannot but admit other human beings must, as inexplicable as it may be, exist. In my heart of hearts I think I am the only thing there is.

The story is going around that Jessica's brother, David, who is thirteen, has been caught, or is accused of, stealing comic books from the drug store – shoplifting. I pay little attention to it until Peter tells me it was all wrong.

"It wasn't David, it was Jessica," he says, "and it wasn't comic books it was chocolate bars. I was watching her. I saw it all."

"How can a story be so far wrong? Wrong person, wrong gender, wrong items. But they don't prosecute children."

"It's zero tolerance, even on shoplifting."

"But she's a girl."

"Oh, her parents will pay for everything. It's the way they raise kids these days. Remember what would have happened to you if you'd been caught stealing?"

"Nothing."

"I would have been whipped with a birch switch."

I was never caught stealing, but my mother caught me drunk once when I was thirteen. She told me she'd move out, that she wasn't going to live with a drunkard. I wasn't a drunkard, I said. Then don't act like one. So I didn't, never again, and yet now she is gone and I could if I wanted to. Robert uses cocaine, though he doesn't think anybody knows. Where does he get it? I don't know. Maybe there's mail order. Maybe from Peter. Peter did time in jail once, for…

What about Robert? Does Robert have violence in him? Enough to warrant watching? One day, perhaps, a drunken or cocainic rage. But I think not. I think he is a good man. One day it will catch up to him, of course, as it does to all. Even good men. We are all good men.

"Pierre, how are you?" John says, "I see you've got some ice cream." I have a plastic spoon and a Styrofoam cup and some French vanilla from Spunkle's Special Treats and I am standing in front of a bench.

"I fixed their leaking tap," I say. "They gave me ice cream."

"Good, good. A hot day, eh?"

"Yes, a hot day."

"Pierre, there's a rumour about you. That you go out at night and walk around."

"Why is that a rumour?"

"That you poke about people's yards. You do go out at night, I know that."

"How do you know that?"

"Because I've seen you."

"Then you must have been out at night."

"Yes, but I was in a car."

He has me there. I have no car.

"Pierre, Pierre, I'm going to ask you this as a friend, and I want you to tell me. Do you spy on people?"

"No," I say, confused, "I watch Jackie."

"Jackie? Jesus, Pierre, why? What do you do? You'll have to stop."

"I worry about her."

"Why?"

"I have to worry about someone."

"Worry about yourself, Pierre. Worry about yourself," and he walks away.

❋

It is raining and I am out in it. I am standing in the rain, just standing in the rain; it's a miserable feeling, I'm soaking again. Let the stormy clouds chase all the sun from the sky, come on with the pain, there's a good reason why I'm standing, just standing in the rain. Actually, I am waiting for the bus. Nobody remembers that movie anymore anyway.

It is not often I take the bus. I am going to Sabreville, the next town over. I am going to watch the Highland Games. Men in kilts with hairy knees and fat muscles. Young, young girls step dancing in short bouncy skirts. Bagpipes. People selling their wares. Artists selling their wares. Their weavings and drawings. What are those shapes in the rain? In the gloom? Who are they? What do they want? They approach. I brace myself. No, no, they are not there. It is…a mirage. That was close. Maybe I shouldn't be here. Maybe I should go home. I go home, walking. I still get wet through. Perhaps the fire next time.

Nine

The paper, *Le Echo*, announces it. It is a story. Not a big enough story to be *the* story, but a story. Gerald no doubt is helping her. Jackie is going to run for mayor. "A Better City For A Better World." She is wrong already. We are not a city. Jackie has no chance. Then again she is an attractive woman, it would be wrong to let her lose. It would be wrong not to vote for her. She may be our Trudeau. Finally, Irving Layton said, Canada has produced a leader worthy of assassination. Gerald has influenced her. She wants to run on a law and order platform.

It is unfair to try. It is unfair to have an ambition. It is unfair to want. It is unfair to see. Vision is cheating. The small bugs, we must keep our eyes on the small bugs, that is where our future lies. The unending war, the unending fascination. Jackie is not going to lose. I am going to lose Jackie. The one person I thought might be...me.

✵

I have been thinking about something. I have been thinking that perhaps I am a bad person. I made Mama's life very hard, I know, and at the end I stood beside her bed with my hands and watched her struggle. I knew there was no point. She gurgled and gasped, panicked, I believe, by her stiffening lungs, the lack of air, her skipping, pausing heart, whatever it was.

She did not speak. I did not speak, though my hands were sweaty. I had not given her her pills that day; things happen, you forget, you get confused, you sleep through, you get angry, you want to win for once but you only hurt yourself when you win.

I fluffed the pillow up afterwards and smoothed it out. I would iron the sheets later, but first they had to be washed. Yes, definitely, first they had to be washed. No one had slept in that bed until Mrs. Bluto came, and she may be dead herself now for all I know – for all I know everyone might be dead. Sitting in that bedroom in a chair beside the bed drinking my cold tea, alone, for all I knew there was no one else alive in the world. How would I know? Perhaps there was only me. Guy was dead, after all, and mother was dead, and Leticia was dead, and whoever the boy was was, and the old man, and my hopes, and my life, and me. But here I am all the same.

I take a breath and decide it is time to take action. I just put off deciding what action to actually take until later, until some other, more advantageous, or at least self-evident, time. Time, as they say, waits for no man – she does, however, give her phone number to anything in pants.

I call John on the phone. "What did you mean," I say, "by what you said?"

"I mean I know what you do, Pierre."

"And I know what you do, John."

"I don't do anything."

"Every Thursday in front of Tapparie Bar at eleven o'clock. A blonde with a limp."

"She's my sister."

"She must be the sister of a lot of men," I say. "She must be from a large family. Many men come to see her there every night."

"A man has the right to what he pays for."

"It's not a crime to be stupid, John. Look at the Pope."

"I won't have you bad-mouth the Holy Father, Pierre. I draw the line at that. I could kill you if I wanted to; who would care? I could turn you in."

"John, I am a fatherless boy."

"You are a cocksucker," he says, and hangs up.

I hold the phone in my hand a long time, and tap it against my forehead.

There is a theme here, I think, and the theme is sex. You can be born male, you can be born female, you can be born both, but can you be born nothing? Neutral: neither at all one nor at all the other? With no hormones, no sexuality, no bits or parts, a sexual void? What would that make you? If your crotch was a smooth round of uninterrupted skin, like a Ken doll, your face and hair androgynous, not too tall or too small, not liking boys or girls or children or animals or magazines. A neutral ground. Would you be human? No. So by doing what I do I defend my humanity, I honour my maker – I do not anger him, he accepts me as I am, he accepts the sacrifice I present – I am being authentic, real, terrible, dog-like and Jezebel, Onan, David, Lot's daughters, Rebekah's older sister, Sodomish, Gomorrahish, Mary Magdalene, the woman taken in adultery, the Jews, the Romans with their bathhouses, the Greeks with their Vice, the hanged man's orgasm (I almost said 'hung'), the sweat that flies off the brow of the man hammering in the nails in the Israeli heat and the flies that seek out the spot.

I kill because I turn down the deal. Because I will not accept what's being offered. I do not assent. You cannot show me any place where I signed on. When I crush a bug or smush a spider, or swat a moth, or pour boiling water on an ant hill, I am saying I may be certain to lose, I am certain to lose, but one of the world's gods will be less an eye.

I take a garden trowel and hold it in my hand in a tight fist. I must go find John. I must find him and give him back his gardening trowel; I do not want it in my house, in my yard, in my dirt. I will throw it at him. I will strike a blow for freedom. I will stun him with it. He thinks he is my friend. I do not want a friend like John. I want a friend like Jesus.

I have on my old shoes, which are mostly uppers, and my eyes itch like crazy. It is the stuff they put on the sides of the road to kill the weeds. It always feels like iodine in the eyes. But it is cheaper than cutting the grass, which says something interesting about the dismal science.

I put sunglasses on and exit past Jock Renard's place next door, on the other side from Mrs. Bluto's place, or former place. Jock is a keep-to-himself, grizzled kind of man, never married, no children. Probably sixty, if he isn't dead and re-animated by some spiteful necromancer. He has a woodpile on his side of our property line and as I pass it, focused on fear and hate, courage and yearning, an awful smell strikes my breath like a rotten cat or a family of cannibal skunks.

That is it, of course: skunks. We have a problem with them around town and around our houses and they have, some, presumably, taken up housing in Renard's old woodpile.

Suddenly, as if the earth has moved during a good-bye, I forget about John, I forget about philosophy, and law, and justice, and humanity, and death by misadventure, or by adventure, or Leticia or Jackie or Guy, and I think, "Those Goddamned skunks are back around here," and I hate them with good old fashioned dog-hate-cat animal instinct. I must get at them. I must root them out.

I can feel my good sense leave me for better quarters elsewhere. But I must do it. I pull logs off, swearing and slashing at them with my trowel until I reach home plate. "Ah," I think, "I see." There are no skunks. There is a piece of shiny metal on a chain. A St. Christopher's medal? No.

The first person I see when I reach downtown is Jackie, but I keep my distance because sometimes the sight or smell of a woman can give a man's brain hiccups. My eyes are already watering. Jackie walks past me without speaking. Perhaps John is spreading rumours about me. Still, you'd think she would have said something.

The next person I see is Robert, looking through one of the trash barrels on the sidewalks. He does that, he told me, because he once found a pile of old *Life* magazines someone had thrown out and he treasured them, so now he can not pass a public trash barrel without checking. How appropriate, I think to myself – in a rubbish barrel.

Ralphie's butcher shop has a 'closed' sign on it even though it should have an 'open' sign. Perhaps Ralphie is sick, or Mrs. Ralphie, or one of the little Ralphettes. Perhaps people have stopped eating meat. Perhaps people have suddenly started wondering why there are no stray cats or dogs around town.

The door to *Chez Louise* is open and there is a portable sign out front that says '50% off'. I wonder if that means the top half or the bottom half of the dress.

I realize I haven't seen Peter in quite awhile.

I pass the school and I know it is just before recess. No one is out. I went to that school, years ago. I walk up to where I can see in the windows. The Art Room is empty but there are childish pictures on the wall. We had to fight to get them to keep art lessons in the curriculum. The board drew the line at gym and music though, and both the physical education and music teachers were let go to save money, and the money saved went where, exactly? No one knows.

In the next classroom there is a class and I recognize Carole by her long dark hair, smartly dressed and sitting paying attention. Then, close to the window where I am, I notice Jessica, looking bored. I tap to get her attention. She looks up and Ms. Button, the teacher, looks and Ms. Button comes over and looks right at me like I have been chewing gum in her class, or in my old teacher's class, who used to be very strict. She draws the curtain.

I shrug and go on. Perhaps Jock, who is the janitor there, will let me in sometime after hours. If I ask him. If I tell him.

After watching the ducks on the river, the brown river – liquefied shit, it looks like, probably is, actually – and getting very hungry, I go to a bench under a tree and take out two slices of buttered bread. I know, I know, but I wanted to try it. I had taken the pound of butter out of the fridge and had to slice it like a bar of soap when I made it. Now it is warm and smooth, but patchy on the bread, little globs, puddles of butter. It tastes salty. Someone has cried on my sandwich.

I can do nothing for a long time, and I do, and when I walk my way back toward where I have come from, there are more people downtown, the regular people, farmers, shoppers, youth, daters, parents with kids, and Jessica Lesser, alone, standing and looking away down the street like she is estimating how much farther she has to go on aching feet. I know the feeling.

I go up to her.

"Jess, my love. How are you, eh? Everything okay?" I say.

She looks torn between a friendly face and a fear, or a duty.

"I'm not supposed to talk to you," she says.

"Oh. Well, I'm sorry to hear that. There's something I need help on, just one thing. I was hoping – don't worry; it is a good thing, a Godly thing. Your parents would approve. I know your Mom and Dad. It is prayer. I know someone who is in trouble, perhaps sick; will you pray with me for him? There is the church. The prayers of a child go straight to heaven they say. More so than my prayers would. Please? In the church?"

Jessica is good, a stalwart girl, yeomanly, even. She would not say no to prayer in a church. I put my hand lightly on her back and guide her forward. She says nothing.

I move my hand up to her hair. "Thank you," I say. "This man is facing great trials."

"I won't know what to pray," she says.

"Little child, God will send you the words."

We pass through a crowd of conversationalists blocking the sidewalk and to do so I take Jessica's hand. The church is large and stone and brownish-beige and steepled and the grass neatly clipped like you never know when someone from out of town is going to come by and want to take a photo of it. Best to put your good foot forward.

Inside all is stone and stained dark brown, wooden pews and pulpit and trim, and the clatter of Jessica's – I almost said 'Leticia's' – hard black shoes on the floor. It is empty.

We go up to the front and I tell her to kneel down, which she does, folding her hands in front of her. I kneel too.

"Dear God," I say, and pause.

"I don't know what to pray," she says. "No one told me."

"Pray that this cup may pass from…alternatively, pray that it does not."

I can hear the main doors behind us open and light enters across our backs. "Hush," I say, "just love," and I take her left hand between my two, flat out, and hold it in a praying position, like the engraving. I can hear a voice. I raise our three hands to my mouth and press my lips against my fingers. There is a rising noise like thunder, gathering, like violent indigestion, like an involuntary, orgasmic squeal.

"There he is," it says.

I hold her hand tighter. There is another voice. "Get him."

Leticia – *Jessica* – stands up, but I hold on to her hand. Someone – it must have been a man – cuffs me on the head, hard, and someone grabs my left arm and pulls me that way. I let go.

"The police."

"They're coming. They're coming."

"Hold him."

"I saw it all."

"Hold him."

"The fucking coward. The fucking coward."

Someone I do not know punches me violently in the stomach.

"Jesus, Jose, no, don't kill him. Leave him for Simon."

I suffer. I have no air, no life. My mouth is full of some unpleasant taste and I try to vomit. Someone pulls my head up by the hair.

Mrs. Lesser walks up to me, and everyone falls quiet. We stare at each other, simply, for what seems like a minute. No one breathes. Then, deliberately, coldly, she raises her right hand, long red fingernails and all, pauses, and then slaps me as hard as I have ever been slapped across the face. This seems to take the anger out of the crowd.

One of her fingernails must have cut me above the eye as I can feel, or think I can feel, a bead of blood on my brow.

"When will Simon come?" I wonder.

Simon comes.

Ten

Constable Simon brings me in in handcuffs and sits me down in a chair opposite a desk in the town's police station. Simon is a middle-aged, usually friendly, but usually serious, policeman. I have no hard feelings.

The man opposite me at the desk is large and doughy and has short stubby hair that I think is probably red, or would be, if it grew. He is evidently of higher rank than Simon, as he sits while Simon stands.

I have been here ten minutes already.

"This, this is a Medic Alert bracelet," the man says, holding up a plastic bag with the metallic medallion and chain, "This was in your pocket. Why? Do you know who it belongs to? It belongs to Philippe Grossman. But you knew that, didn't you? Because you took him off the beach where he was with his parents…"

"Naked," I say. "I read it in the papers."

"Did he give you this? Did you take it? Answer me. Do you know the penalty for murder?"

Do I know the penalty for murder? I think. Of course I know the penalty for murder: being a murderer.

"Where did you get this, eh?"

"The wood pile in Jock Renard's yard."

"Really, now? Tell me, Constable Simon, you just came from there. Is there a wood pile in Jock Renard's yard?"

"Not that I saw," Simon says.

"I cleaned it up."

"What did you do with it?"

"I burnt it in my fireplace."

"In this heat?"

"I didn't want…"

"What? What didn't you want, eh?"

"Things hide in there, injured and when they're sick or dead. Then they smell and the rats come, and the rats eat them and they spread disease so that more things get sick and die in the wood pile and the rats have more to eat, so there are more rats and more rats, and why would I want that to happen to the world?"

"Jock Renard has an alibi."

"Is it a good one?"

"No."

The officer stands up. "But he is not a pervert. He does not walk around with a murdered boy's bracelet in his pocket, he does not peek in school windows and he does not try to take away a young girl, and he does not sneak and snoop around all night, and he is not sitting here in my police station for trying to do God knows what. And you are."

There is nothing I can say to that.

"Listen, Pierre, I like you. You're a good fellow. It's not your fault. It's an illness. It's an illness and we can get you help. You'd like that, wouldn't you? Someplace quiet for a while, where you'll be safe. Just tell us, just say it."

Simon speaks in the ear of the officer who is interviewing me. I can hear what he says. Perhaps he means me to. He says, "The Lessers want to press charges. They insist. The public is with them. There is a crowd outside."

"You see, Pierre, you see what you've done? Now you've gotten me in trouble. Is that fair? I ask you, is it fair? To get me in trouble? What are you going to do, Pierre?"

Directly across from me, over the officer's head on the wall behind him, is a calendar of female nudes. Ms. August is naked on a treadmill. She looks Swedish to me. Why is it there are so few black female nudes, I wonder? I am always curious about black women. Do they get tan lines?

"What do you dream about?" I ask the officer.

"Dreams? You have dreams? Fantasies, eh? Tell me about your fantasies, Pierre. Are they sexual? You like young girls? School girls? Everyone likes high school girls, don't worry. Their uniforms, their hair, it's natural. But children, Pierre, that is where we have to draw the line. Understand me Pierre, I have sworn to protect the people – the children – of this community. And I will."

Personally, I do not daydream about sex, though no one will believe me. My fantasies, though, are full of conversations. People talking to me. Me talking to people. Long, elaborate, warm, meaningful, spontaneous conversations. Easy talk. The person I am talking to likes me, picks up on all the obscure cultural references I have acquired. Talk, just talk. Connection. Prayer.

"You raped and murdered Leticia Carmichael. You did God knows what to Philippe Grossman on that beach. You tried to abduct Jessica Lesser. Admit it. And you spied on Jackie Thomas in her own bedroom. And you spied on midnight bathers – probably skinny dippers – on the beaches. I'm asking you one last time, will you sign a confession? There are people out there."

Anyone might turn lead into gold, or walk on Mars someday, find the missing link, discover the unified field theory, prove God. Anyone might, at any moment – it may happen. But the truth is, it hasn't happened yet, and that is what we must live with.

There is a story of a man who killed himself in despair when the young girl he loved married another man. This is an old story. Chinese or Indian or something. And the dead man was reincarnated as the only child of his love and her more successful suitor. And like any good mother, the woman loved her child more than she loved her husband.

I consider my options. One word and all will be all right. One word and the Christ child can be born. And the world can go on sinning and being saved, sinning and being saved. What is that word? Yes. What is that magic phrase that makes life worth living? "I do," I say.

"You do what?"

"Want to confess."

"To what?"

"Your choice. Anything...everything."

✵

It occurs to me, riding to the city in the back of a police car, handcuffed, to wonder what Jock Renard is doing, or will be doing again, sly devil, sinner that he is. Or Robert, addict and sleepless man of the people, will he turn to drink as well and dissolve? Peter the ex-convict. John and his lame-legged prostitute, a sordid, a dangerous, a weakened thing – capitalism in its purest form. Jackie and her life from man to man, saddened or relieved each time, growing older, wider, greyer; ultimately the game always gets called on account of darkness and when the old look in the mirror they see what they will look like dead.

Ralphie and his disappearing business. Maybelle and her pink little girl dresses. Jessica, so always unsure, so always confused. Carole, bold, a child who will look you in the eye. Uncle Jacob, a man I believe truly capable of murders. Could be dealing drugs, probably to Robert. The lumberjacks in the mountains, the women like Laura who hang around graveyards, the nude sunbathers with breasts the colour of porn stars. Me. Them. God. The rabbits hit by trucks on our highways.

The time has come, the Walrus said. It is more right now than it ever will be again, this time. I will stand in the box and all eyes will be on me and I will swallow with my dry mouth and have my moment, enjoy my moment, a moment of such rightness, of such oneness, of such fixedness and I will be brave and happy, the tether around my body like God's Plumb Line and God will smile at me and I will finally have done what I always said I would give anything to do – give the universe a good feeling, a breath, a chaste kiss, a holiday, an extended holiday, from all the things, the very things, I know. I am not the son of man. I am the son of Giselle Creamer, guardian of Guy, friend of Leticia, former neighbour of Mrs. Bluto, neighbour of Jock Renard – child killer that he is. Christian agnostic, fool, small, small man, bug, yet even I, even I – it will happen to me, through me.

I am going to Montreal to be judged and sentenced. The highway scenery flashes by like warrior stones. I am on stage. How happy I am, how apropos, all those lives snuffed out like a candle. It is better to light than to curse the darkness which is blown out only when the sun rises.

Ultimately there is no reason for things. People just are. It is not a bad thing to be alive. It is not such a bad thing to live out your life – even in prison. I look out the window at the other cars, all going in the other direction. After all, I think, how much worse can it be?

The officer in the front turns and looks at me. "Scum," he says.

Other Quattro Novellas

Shrinking Violets by Heidi Greco
The Panic Button by Koom Kankesan
Grace by Vanessa Smith
Retina Green by Reinhard Filter
Gaze by Keith Cadieux
Tobacco Wars by Paul Seesequasis
The Sea by Amela Marin
Real Gone by Jim Christy
A Gardener on the Moon by Carole Giangrande
Good Evening Central Laundromat, by Jason Heroux
Of All the Ways To Die by Brenda Niskala
The Cousin by John Calabro,
Harbour View by Binnie Brennan
The Extraordinary Event of Pia H. by Nicola Vulpe
A Pleasant Vertigo by Egidio Coccimiglio
Wit in Love by Sky Gilbert
The Adventures of Micah Mushmelon by Michael Wex
Room Tone by Gale Zoë Garnett